This bucket belongs to:

- - - - - - - - - - - -

For our two mini baby Bells

First published in Great Britain by Beachy Books in 2009

For more information visit
www.beachybooks.com

ISBN: 978-0-9562980-0-3

Jack & Boo's
Bucket
of
Treasures

Written by **Philip Bell**   Illustrated by **Eleanor Bell**

Beachy Books
www.beachybooks.com

On my beach
I slip-slide down
mountains of pebbles
piled high by waves
towards the low tide
in search of treasure
gifts from the sea.

I spot sea glass
for my bucket
sandblasted
in storms
a lost jewel
from a mermaid's
purse.

Seaglass

Through a hole
in a lucky
hag stone
I spy seagulls
circling high
hovering
on the wind.

Hag Stone

Herring Gull

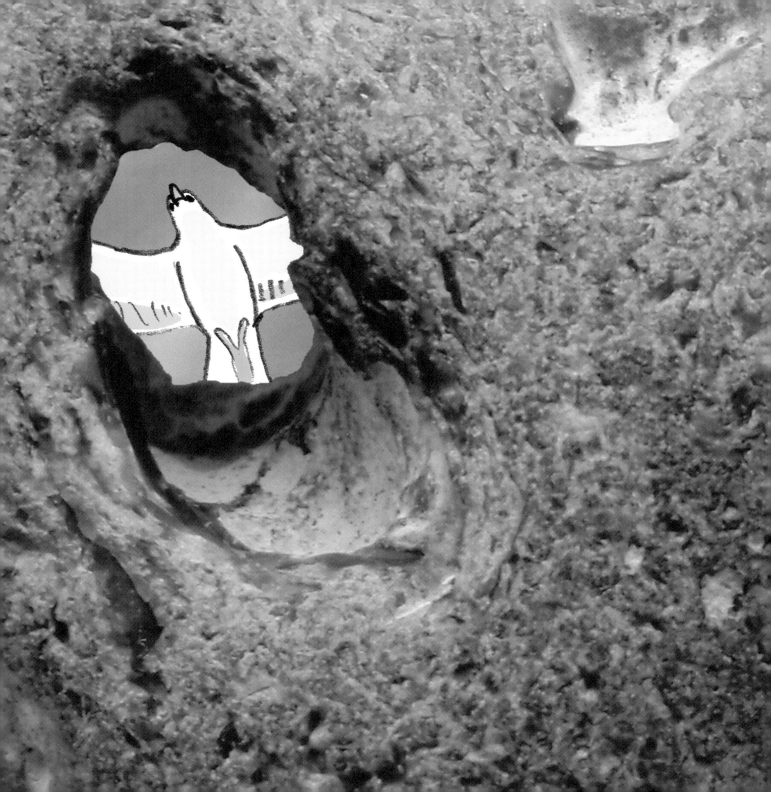

Ahoy ye salty seadogs!

On Captain's orders
I walk the plank
across driftwood
from a sunken
pirate's ship.

Socks off and my toes
sink into muddy sand
squelch squelch
and my feet
are buried
deeper than lugworms.

lugworm
cast in
sand

I step on
slippery rocks
growing green
stringy seaweed hair.

I step over
crowds of barnacles
and silent mussels
waiting
for tide's return.

Mussel

As I look for crabs in a
shimmering rock pool
my shadow disturbs
a little green fish.

Boo touches a sticky sea
anemone. She squeals as
the tentacles stick to her
fingers.

Blenny –
a rockpool fish

Velvet swimming crab

I splash through
snaking streams
trickling
into the sea.

I pick up
bladderwrack
and pop its
air sacs.

We race into the sea
and scream when chilly
waves crash over our legs.

Under my fingers
I find a hidden shell
buried in the sand.

common whelk

slipper limpet

The sun sets
behind Beachy Head
as waves climb
higher up the shore
laden with fresh secrets.

Wrapped in a warm
towel I look south and
thank the sea for my
bucket of treasures.

Beach Spotter Guide

Hag Stone

Velvet swimming crab

Rope

lugworm cast in sand

Mussel

common whelk

Seaglass

Slipper limpet

Blenny
a rockpool fish
Also called a
Shanny

Hermit crab

Mermaid's
purse or
egg case

(if you find one
records should be
sent to the shark Trust
www.eggcase.org)

Cuttlefish
bone

Whelk eggs

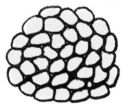

Herring Gull

Common
periwinkle

Family Beach Ideas

Collect your own Bucket of Treasures

Comb the beach, explore rock pools and dig in the sand. Remember to leave wildlife as you find it after your adventures.

Stone Skimming and Pebble Plopping

Find flat smooth pebbles and spin your "skimmer" out at the sea and count the bounces. Keep it in line with the horizon and as low to the waves as possible. Or for younger ones, just throw pebbles out to sea and listen for the fun "plop" noise!

Eat Fish and Chips for Tea

Eat them hot, straight out of the bag, sitting on the beach. Buy sustainable, locally caught, fresh fish. Look out for fish certified by the Marine Stewardship Council (MSC).

Defend your Sandcastle from the Sea

Build a sandcastle close to the shoreline, dig a moat around it and create a channel from it down to the sea. Then wait for the tide to come in and watch as your moat fills up. As the sea rolls in, try to block off the channel with wet sand and see how long you can hold back the tide from destroying your castle.

Beachy Art

Use empty shells, string, driftwood and other beach finds to create a seaside collage. Collect different shades of pebbles and use them to create letters on the beach. Smooth damp sand makes a great canvas for massive messages and drawings you can see from the sky.

Have fun and play safe on the beach!

Visit www.beachybooks.com to find out more about Jack & Boo's adventures...

LaVergne, TN USA
30 November 2009
1636LVUK00002B